THE STORY OF TH LITTLE RED ENGINE

Pictures by
Leslie Wood

Story by
Diana Ross

ANDRE DEUTSCH
CLASSICS

First published in Great Britain in 1945 by Faber and Faber Ltd.

This edition published in 1999 by André Deutsch Classics.

All rights reserved. Text © 1945 Diana Ross. Illustrations © Elsie Wood.

ISBN 0 233 99402 5.

Once upon a time there was a Little Red Engine. It lived in a big shed beside the station of Taddlecombe Junction, and every day at seven o'clock it came out of its shed to go on its journey.

As it left the station it would give a loud whistle, and that meant, "Goodbye! Goodbye! It's seven o'clock, it's time to go! Goodbye! Goodbye!" and away it would go – dig-a-dig dig, dig-a-dig dig, dig-a-dig dig, all the way to Dodge, Mazy, Callington Humble, Never Over, Soke, Seven Sisters, Dumble and home.

Now first it would pass by the Jubilee cottages and old
Mrs Ransom's little dog Hurry would come running out
every morning and:

"Bow wow wow," he would cry. "Good morning,
Little Red Engine."

And the Little Red Engine would give a whistle,
WHOOEOO, "Good morning, little dog Hurry,"
and on it would go with a dig-a-dig dig.

And then it would pass old Gregory's farmyard and all the ducks on the pond would cry, "Quack, Quack, Quack! Good morning, Little Red Engine!"

And the Little Red Engine would give a whistle, WHOOEOO, "Good morning, Good morning," and on it would go with a dig-a-dig dig.

And then it would go by Callington Manor, and the Baronet's donkey would cry, "EE-AW! EE-AW! Good morning, Little Red Engine!"

And the Little Red Engine would reply, WHOOEOO, "Good morning, Neddy,"

and would hurry along with a dig-a-dig dig.

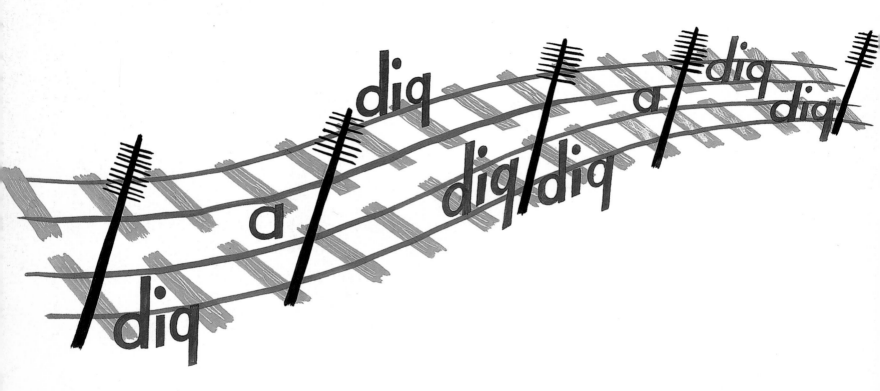

And when it ran through Seldom Spinney the gamekeeper's
cat, who had only one eye, would jump through the wire and cry:
"Miaow, Miaow! Good morning, Little Red Engine!"

And the Little Red Engine would say WHOOEOO, "Good morning to you," and on it would go with a dig-a-dig dig.

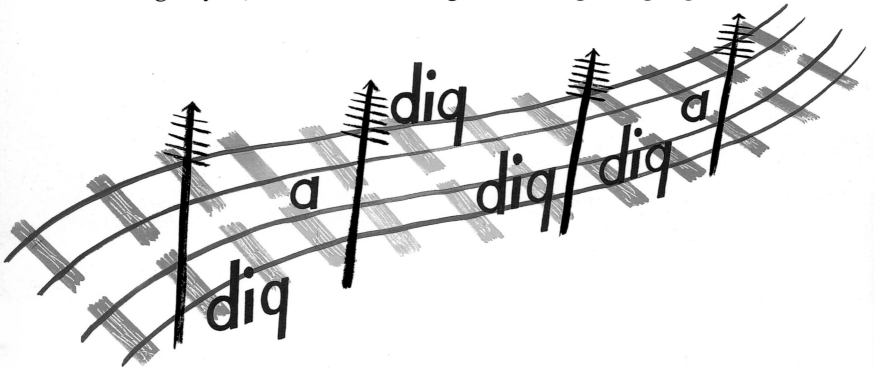

At Merrymans Rising the Little Red Engine would change its tune, and instead of dig-a-dig dig it would go chuffa chuffa chuffa chuff, chuffa chuffa chuffa chuff, while the sheep who

grazed on the hillside would stop their eating and would all turn towards it and cry:

"Baa Baa, Good morning, Little Red Engine!"

The Little Red Engine would say nothing till it got to the top

and then it would let out SUCH a whistle:
WHOOEOOEOO, "I've done it, I've done it,
Good morning, Goodbye," and down the other
side it would go, dig-a-dig dig as fast as you please.

And last of all, at Noman's Puddle the frogs, when they heard it coming, would poke their heads out of the marshes and sing:

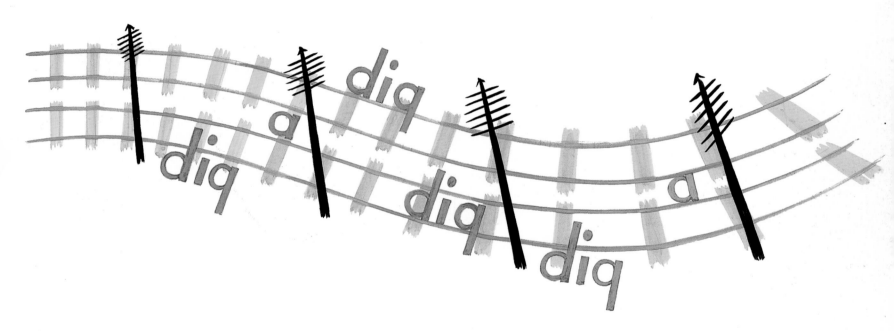

REK KEK KEK KEX, REK KEK KEK KEX as loud as they could...

"Good morning, Little Red Engine."
And the Little Red Engine would whistle
WHOOEOO, "Thank you very
much." But it didn't really think the frogs
had very nice voices.

And besides all this, at each one of the ten level-crossings
there was always a chance of a car. And the cars would go:
UUR UUR UUUR as cars will, "Hurry up and let
me through."

And the Little Red Engine would hurry up and
the cars would toot "Thank you," and the Little Red Engine would
whistle WHOOEOO and on it would go with a dig-a-dig dig.

But now, one morning, whatever was this? At seven o'clock no Little Red Engine! Mrs Ransom's Hurry barked, "Bow WOW WOW. It's never been late before!"

Farmer Gregory's ducks went "QUACK QUACK QUACK. Whatever can have happened?"

The Baronet's donkey cried "EE-AW EE-AW. I'd never have thought it!"

The Gamekeeper's cat said "Miaow, Miaow, there's no knowing these days."

And the sheep on the hillside said "BAA BAA. Things are not what they were."

And as for the frogs on Noman's Puddle, they made such a racket and a croaking that you couldn't distinguish a word they said; whilst the cars went whizzing over the crossings, surprised that no one stopped them.

And what had happened to the Little Red Engine? The Little Red Engine was ill!

At half past six its driver had come and had cleaned it and polished it and stoked it and got up steam, but when he took the brakes off,

SHHHHH sighed the Little Red Engine and did not move.

The driver tried again.

Chuffa Chuffa SHHHHHHH. The Little Red Engine could not go!

They ran for the mechanic and told him what had happened. "The Little Red Engine is ill, can you come and make it better?" The mechanic came to the shed and looked at the Little Red Engine. He looked at it inside and he looked at it outside. He looked very wise. Off he went and came back with a can.

"Here is the medicine to make it better. Twice a day and don't forget." And what do you think the medicine was called? OIL!

The driver took the medicine and gave it to the Little
Red Engine and no sooner did it taste it than...

Dig-a-dig dig, Dig-a-dig dig, they could hardly keep it on the lines! "We are late this morning. Make up for lost time," and away it went...

...dig-a-dig dig, dig-a-dig dig, dig-a-dig dig, faster than ever before.

As it passed the cottages, "Woof, WOOF WOOF, whatever was the matter?"

"Sorry to be late, sorry to be late," and the Little Red Engine was gone.

It rushed by the duck pond. "QUACK QUACK QUACK QUACK. You've come at last!"

"Sorry to be late, sorry to be late," and the Little Red Engine was gone!

The Baronet's donkey cried "EW-AW EE-AW, I thought you were shirking."

"Sorry to be late, sorry to be late,"

and there it was climbing Merrymans Rising without ever a pause to change its tune.

"BAA BAA BAA, you can't keep it up, you can't keep it up."

But the Little Red Engine was down the other side before the sheep had even stopped speaking. And when the frogs saw it coming they waved their legs in the air:

"Here comes old lightning! Here comes the Flying Scotsman! REK KEK KEK KEX, REK KEK KEK KEX."

And as for the cars at the crossings, they had no time to say "Hurry". The Little Red Engine was by them before ever they had uttered a toot. And there it was, home in the shed not one minute later than usual!

"You certainly are SOME engine," said the driver patting it proudly, and he gave it some medicine, and the Little Red Engine sighed a gentle little whistle, WHOOEOO, and went happily to sleep.

THE END